Tough and Tender:
The Crybaby Collective Volume Two

TOUGH AND TENDER
VOLUME 2

The Crybaby Club Artist & Author Collective

the crybaby club
2018

First Printing: 2018

ISBN 978-0-9986395-3-6

The Crybaby Club: Artist & Authors Collective
PO Box 40147
Memphis, Tennessee 38174

www.heycrybaby.com

Ordering Information:
Special discounts are available on quantity purchases by corporations, associations, educators, and others. For details, contact the publisher at the above listed address.

Contents

Introduction

Dearest You,

First of all, thank you for reading this work. Everyone involved is very excited about it, and when you purchase or read through Tough & Tender you are supporting not just a dream; but a bunch of dreams all over the world coming true - and *that* is invaluable. So of course, I am grateful and so happy that you are reading this.

When I founded The Crybaby Club in January 2016, I had no idea where it would lead. I had no plan, no expectations, no idea at the reach I would attain, the community I would build and the message that would resonate with so many.

My ideas of being emotionally self-aware and unapologetic with your feelings combined with feminism, cute art and radical softness swept across the world thanks to the wonder that is social media, and took me on this magical ride. A ride that led to a book! An anthology based off my initial idea, and carried out by lovely humans who believed in it and wanted to have a part in it.

This book is dedicated to them.

This book is dedicated to you.

This book is dedicated to anyone who has ever cried, and felt ashamed of it.

This book is for the crybabies and those who love us.
We love you too.

Natalie Meagan
Founder and Creative Director of The Crybaby Club

Chapter One
Loss and Tears

Happy Tears
by Eileen Ramos

Recently I've noticed that I've cried and teared up now more than ever before. I'm not sure if it was due to the incredible Crybaby Club, where I have witnessed so many people open up about their life and vulnerabilities. Where I finally found a place I can freely admit my mental illness struggles, and not feel alone. Or maybe it's because I'm more acclimated to my medicine nowadays and just able to feel more. In any case, I'm thankful for both: to have a sanctuary where I can absolutely be myself when society wants a happy, static mask; and to have dosages that allow me feel more human and "normal".

This past year I have had more happy tears than sad ones - at least four to one. I never imagined I could be so joyful about crying, but here I am actually tearing up from realizing that I'm truly ecstatic to be alive and to be *me*. An emotion I was never able to find when I was suicidal for years, and deeply immersed in self-loathing, guilt, and regret. Now, I no longer feel those heavy weights, and every single day I love myself more and more.

Dear reader, I want to share with you a list of my happiest tears and another of what I hope will be my reasons for crying in the future. I wish you lengthy lists, realized dreams, and bright hopes. You deserve to be happy.

Let no one else tell you different.

I was so happy, I cried, because:

1. I held the hands of my queer role model, Be Steadwell, during the first time we met at a film screening. She's a fantastic, black DIY pop singer who I loved even before I realized I was bi. While she hugged me, I tearfully told her how she inspired me to be me, to be as creative as possible, to love

freely, and to challenge myself to be a better artist and individual. I told her how much she meant to me as a fellow woman of color and that I couldn't be the only one who felt this way because of her. She would try to catch my eye while I was tearing and silent and asked me what was wrong, but I just told her how happy I was to be there with her. I told her that I felt alone, but she told me that I no longer was - because the audience was my family, and that they were here for me. She will always be my heroine.

2. I finally had a breakthrough during rehearsing my monologue about my psychotic break. These tears were initially sad, but they became happy when my director, Summer, told me she knew I could do it and how powerful my words were. I cried harder when she hugged me when I needed it. She was the first person to believe I could perform, an art form that I truly thought were beyond my capabilities. She was also the first person to publish my words in a book, a feat I never thought feasible.

3. After the final show where I performed that monologue, I went up to Summer and thanked her for always believing in me when I never could. For pushing me to get onstage and become the mental health advocate I always wanted to find. She cried too.

4. That monologue contained secrets I never dared to utter for years; and to express aloud my worst delusions, fears, and experiences was the ultimate catharsis. I witnessed people crying during my performance - including strangers, family, and close friends. They'd all come up to me to thank me for stating my truth, how necessary it was, and how much support it will build in the community. I cried when I realized that this was the path and vocation I needed to stay on.

5. On my 29th birthday, an internet friend I barely know or even talked to posted this on my Facebook wall: "Hope you are

struck still for a minute by the fact that you have touched and comforted the souls of many.... that you do not even know!" And I was, for at least five minutes. I don't know if I'll ever get over that.

6. A year ago I wrote a long public status update on my fears of mania and psychosis - to encourage myself, weeks before I debuted my monologue. Here's the excerpt that made me tear up the most when it popped up on "On This Day":

"I just want to tell "little one" (what the nurses called me in the hospital mental wing) that she will go on to do amazing, significant, and oh so necessary endeavors. That she was meant for so much fucking more than itchy hospital sheets and missing Shrek puzzle pieces.

There's so much more waiting for you, hoping for your arrival. The pain and the hurt and that terrible fear will remain with you. There's no shaking off of those seared, disturbing images in your head. You will think about them every day of your life.

But that doesn't mean that's what will make up your entire world. It's a part of you, but not all of you.

And you're learning to love the difference...

You're resilient. And you'll always be. You're loving, vulnerable, open, and so passionate. You're eloquent and brilliant as well. You're sweet and strong. You have a bright smile and you're really sincere. And you have a good heart at the end of the day.

Don't forget. You've always had these qualities. It just took you too long to realize it."

7. And Summer's comment on the same post made me lose it:

"Eileen, this was so powerful. You are amazing in so many ways. You are first of all an incredibly talented writer. You are prolific, your words are wise and bright and brave, your understanding of and love for language is a rare gem. You're also just amazing as a person. You are passionate, kind, daring and mindblowingly resilient. I know people who haven't even been through half of what you've been through who have totally crumbled.

Your words and your frank discussion of mental illness and all its symptoms - mania included - are breaking ground for people who need to hear these words the most. You are changing the world, Eileen.

Thank you for all you do. You can get through the mania, and through the depression. I know not everyone is religious, but I am, and I believe God never gives us more than we can handle -- and girl, that means you are one of the biggest badasses I know!"

I hope to God that I will always keep her words true.

8. Finally, I cried when I became a bookseller at my favorite bookshop, a true childhood dream come true. I'm surrounded by such supportive and cool co-workers, introduced to fantastic tomes I wouldn't have found otherwise, and get to take home the advance reader copies of adored authors. I'm learning new skills while growing as a person and as a worker. It's pure joy to be able to discuss books with fellow word nerds and introduce customers to their new favorites. I love being here, and I hope I don't lose sight of how much this reality means to me.

I hope I cry over:

1. The first time I say "I love you" to my future partner. I have never said it to anyone in a romantic sense and I take strange pride in that. May I one day drop the arrogance and admit true love.

2. When I realize I'm pregnant for the first time. No matter what I write or where I'm published, my children will be my greatest creations.

3. Slow dancing - I haven't slow danced since I was in middle school and I've been waiting over half my life to be in someone's swaying arms again. Let me cry when I'm dancing with the only partner I'd ever want to serenade Boyz II Men to.

4. Receiving an email from a literary agent who wholeheartedly believes in my words and my work and wants me as their client.

5. Witnessing my baby sister getting married to her true love.

6. Seeing my name in the acknowledgements of a book written by a talented friend who I always believed in, even when they didn't.

7. Finally holding the published book I worked on, dreamed about, and hoped for for so many years.

8. Upon reading a fan letter whose author thanks me for writing the words they needed to hear.

9. Watching a close friend finally and truly be happy and admitting it, when they once confessed they wanted to die.

Self Soothing
by Rhea Smith

I'm living, I'm breathing.
My heart is still beating.
So why, body, do you cry?
Why do you think we'll die?
Please, stop your trembling.
Try and slow your breathing.
Believe we'll be okay.
We will get through today.
Don't worry about my fingers,
They tingle because of panic.
Hyperventilating, 'freaking out'
Thoughts that made you manic.
You'll be okay, I'll be okay.
We will get through today.

Waves
by Meg Colt

They say that grief comes in waves,
but for me there is no ebb and flow.

It's more of a heartbeat,
a steady rhythm,
a ticking reminder
of your absence.

It's that whisper of
what could've been
that always knocks
me over.

"IT'S THE WHISPER
OF WHAT COULD
HAVE BEEN
THAT ALWAYS
KNOCKS ME
OVER."

— MEG COLT

Solutions
by Cassandra Bankson

The anchor lodged in my mind
is heavier than all the joys of the world combined
and succumbing to the ocean seems only sensible
to my lungs protest
I would much rather trade air
for water
Living is comprised of many difficult gulps
but death is only one

For Bailey
(09/04/06 - 09/09/17)
by Rebecca Foley

All I want to do is wrap my arms around you and bury my head in your soft, golden fur. I want to feel your fur between my fingers and your heartbeat under my palm. I want to rub your silky-smooth, floppy ears. I want you to lick my face and I want to kiss those ears.

But I can't.

I still come through the front door and expect to see you running towards me, happy to see me, with your not-so-pearly, white-toothed grin. I still expect to hear your accompanying whine, as you tell me about the day I missed and how you missed me.

But I won't.

When I accidentally drop food on the floor, a noodle, popcorn, or even some chicken, I almost call for "clean up". During a thunderstorm, as thunder roars, I think to look for you and make sure you aren't scared. For a moment, I almost call out your name.

But I don't.

I think about the day you left; being told you had cancer, as you struggled to breathe. I wonder almost every day whether or not there was a way I could have saved you from going through that pain. Saved you from leaving.

But I couldn't.

I tell myself that I've accepted that you're never going to be there when I walk through the door; we will never go on a walk together again, and I will never receive another kiss from you or feel your soft fur through my fingers.

But I haven't.

I don't want to be sad when I think of you. It's hard to think happily about our memories together, when they are only memories and no longer possible. I want to be able to think of you and smile, not just cry at the mere mention of your name.

But I will cry, I will miss, I will love, and one day I will smile.

Because you were not only my dog, but my best friend.

"BUT i WILL CRY,
i WILL MiSS,
i WILL LOVE,
AND ONE DAY
i WILL SMILE."

– REBECCA FOLEY

Anxiety?
by Rhea Smith

I find myself lacking motivation.
I can't tell you how much I hate the sensation.
I'd pay with my life for the fleeting elation…
But that's cheating, isn't it?
I feel pressure pressing down on my entire self.
A list of things to do lays on my shelf.
I don't even feel sorry for myself;
It's just life weighing me down.
No desire rests in my chest,
And a repetitive history dictates the rest.
I'll sit here another while in this mess,
Until it overwhelms my being overwhelmed.

Loss
by Charity Blaine

I had thought that I would write an excerpt about what it felt like losing my dad when I was only seventeen years old, and how I still miss his presence at every milestone, accomplishment, and heartbreak. I realized though: there was a time that loss spoke to me just as clearly, but it taught me more about the strength of the human spirit than my own loss had in all these years.

Olive Daisy was a few years younger than me, a wild artist, who was so seriously introverted that she would disappear into her thoughts for months at a time. She married a boy at her church. Jason was a few years younger than her, from the same group of friends, but very structured, financially wise, and opinionated.

I may not have understood Jason, but I loved Olive like a sister. I had guessed she was pregnant before she even told me. She said she had been sick in the shower a few days in a row. I whispered excitedly, "Olive! Could you be pregnant?" She pulled out an ultrasound, just as I asked. I was confused, it was too early for an ultrasound.

She explained that they had been worried it was an ectopic pregnancy, so they had done some early tests. Everything was fine, although I could tell Olive was nervous. Her plan had been to go back to school, she had done a year of college, but she loved art and wanted to keep learning.

"This wasn't planned, I just forgot to take birth control for two days, but Jason will be so happy. He really wanted to start a family."

The next time I saw her, she was more at peace with what was coming. The time after that, she was getting excited.

Eventually, she and Jason booked me to do maternity photos. She tied a big blue bow around her belly. When Jason leaned in to kiss her, they looked genuinely in love with each other and the baby they had considered naming Charlie.

Then, a day before her due date, the baby died. She stopped feeling him move and when she went to the doctor, they couldn't find a heartbeat. She stayed in the hospital overnight and after eighteen hours of labor, a lifeless baby boy came into the world, surrounded by his loving parents, grandparents, aunts and uncles; christened by their tears. He was chubby, with a little bit of hair and the kind of delicate hands with long fingers that people always admire and say, "He will definitely be a piano player!".

The nurses tenderly put paint on his feet and hands, and placed them against paper to make tiny prints. They made a little bracelet that spelled out "Charlie" and gave it to Olive. They were so kind and loving and cried with her, but could not bring the little baby back to life.

A few days later, I visited Olive at home. Jason sat on the porch writing in a notebook. He looked up to greet me, and I offered my condolences, but I knew they were meaningless beyond the intent. His face was hard to look at, because the pained expression didn't match the youthful face. They did not belong together. He'd barely experienced life, yet he knew the pain of losing a child.

Olive was inside, putting on the kettle. Her body still looked pregnant, which I should have known, but for which I wasn't prepared. I hugged her tight and she cried, and I gave her the yellow daisies I had brought, even though now, seeing her, the flowers seemed so trivial. She showed me the little box that the hospital had gifted to her in Charlie's memory; it contained the bracelet, the footprints and a copy of her ultrasound. She explained each item, and how grateful she was to have them. She told me that her and Jason were taking turns writing in a journal to help process their feelings. She reassured me that she was strong and knew Charlie was in Heaven. Everything I saw in her face was pain and I could feel how much I would ache if I was in her place, and even then she amazed me with her beauty and strength.

"This is really hard, we were so ready to have him in our lives. But I know I'm not alone. My friend Jen, she lost her cousin - and you, you lost your dad. What I went through wasn't as hard as that. We never had a chance to know Charlie, so we don't know what we're missing. You knew your dad and loved him. And I just think about that. And I feel so bad for you, knowing what I know now. And how much Jen loved Ellen. They were best friends, and Jen is so depressed without her. That's worse you know?"

I didn't know, I didn't believe for one second that my suffering was more difficult than hers. But all I could say was, "Oh Olive! I love you so much."

And I did love her. And I never want to forget her compassion at that moment, and her strength in the face of loss. That is the human spirit.

Untitled I
by Cassandra Bankson

I was shattered into countless pieces
and whenever I tried to reconstruct myself
the glue was a weak replacement
For the newly acquired space
I continued to fix the habits
that I tried so hard to break
I sliced my hands a million times over
until it felt painful not to be cut
It's why loving you
is so damn torturous.

Chapter Two
Laughs and Loyalty

Glimmer
by Suzanna Valentine Moore

My brother had the greatest power to make me laugh. More than anyone. We would be sitting at the dinner table and the slightest thing from him would send me into hysterics. For a wisp of a child, I had a big, boisterous laugh. Something you would expect from an elderly man watching the world change. Except I had such little control. My laughter would toss me out of my chair, turn my face beet red, and my family would always respond with a chorus of,

BREATHE!

BREATHE, SUZANNA!

Which, of course, only made things worse. My brother looked at me with that glimmer in his eyes and my laughter turned silent - shaking my whole body, my tiny gaping mouth finally letting out a tangible gasp. My mother let out a sigh of relief.

My brother had this air about him; he always reminded me of Jim Carrey. He could be comical with his whole body or just the slightest expression. He could be so absurd, but he was so brilliant. So genuine. Even physically, with his dark brown hair and eventual beard like Jim's. And that glimmer. He could crack me up with one look, it was almost dangerous.

As we grew up, his power to make me laugh waned. He and I were alike in that we took on the weight of the world - sometimes bringing us closer together, sometimes tearing us apart. His glimmer faded. It came back occasionally when he was pursuing something with his entire being, and it felt like he couldn't be stopped. Like the time he purged everything he owned, bought a motorcycle, and set out around the country.

His power and his influence over me changed as he did. He would give me his favorite book, look me right in the eye, and tell me how important it was that I read it. When I missed him, I could smell his hand-rolled cigarettes that he told me to never smoke. He became so serious, and so passionate. And in that sense, he still reminded me of Jim. My brother became so invested in causes, would wax philosophical for hours if given the chance. He was so engaging, it was easy to give him that attention. He held you in the glimmer in his dark eyes, and he kept you there.

Time passed, and a space grew between us that could never fully be bridged. His cause turned into his God, and it was then that his power over me stopped. He tried to wield it, but I wasn't his impressionable little sister anymore. It was a freeing and unfortunate turning point in my life, the day I realized this. His passions no longer dictated mine. The books he gave me, the ones that molded and shaped me, didn't even match his ideology anymore. I had my own passions, my own pursuits. He helped create a glimmer in me that he no longer had. But, despite who we've become, I see that glimmer in his children's eyes. I hear my own terrible, wonderful laugh in them. For that, I'm forever nostalgic. I hope they hold onto that glimmer for as long as they can.

Untitled II
by Cassandra Bankson

may I take
the time to express
a minuscule token
of my appreciativeness
I am so grateful
of things that seem
just like any other
part of a daily routine.
From birds that chirp
at a sun that will rise
from loving the lack of space
between my thighs
the warmth of a blanket
or kittens purr,
if you stop to listen,
you'll surely concur.
From the radiating smile
of passerby,
to the simple ability
to contemplate why
things are not
always as they seem
and have the open-mindedness
to read the lines in-between.
From buds that blossom
without being asked,
to the winds that kiss
a sailboat's mast
to take someone home
or across immense seas,
to navigate the beauty
within you and me.
And perhaps it takes
loss or failure to see
the apparent love

of friends and family
when hard times test
true love shows through.
I hope you know
I appreciate you
(and all that you do!)

Good Boy
by Caz Brett

My best friend is loyal to a fault.
My best friend is always there when I call him.
He's always there when I don't.
When I'm alone, he follows me around, wordless, always silent,
but his silence speaks volumes to me.

He likes to dig all kinds of holes
some small, some large,
some sturdy, some precarious,
but he doesn't like to bury.
No, he likes to uncover things and share them with me.
Maybe it's something I'm curious in
Maybe it's something I tried to conceal a long time ago.
He doesn't care. He digs them out and he waits.
Waits to see how I'll manage.
Waits to see what I'll do next.
He sits next to me in reticence whilst I figure it all out.

Sometimes we hang out together
Even when I don't want to
When I don't feel ready and I don't feel strong
and he insists that I pay attention to him.

Sometimes when friends are there he sits behind me
His hot, sticky breath on the back of my neck
Someone recounts a story but I just can't focus.
I turn around and he's there, staring at me.

Sometimes he rips up my life to its roots.
Sometimes I wish he didn't exist.
But I'm used to this feeling now.

The medical professionals have bad news
They can help, but there is a catch.

They say: We need to put him down.

They reel off the -omodols and the -odines and the -oprams
but I'm too numb to hear them.
I'm hit by a grief, so great and so sudden.
They will send him to sleep,
make him dormant, inactive.

I imagine my life without him and I cry.
Who will unbury my past mistakes?
Who will torment me at night
and keep my thoughts a blur until the early hours?
Who will follow me with every step
And bite at my ankles at every dinner party?
Who will remind me that I am still here,
still alive, despite the odds?

My best friend is loyal to a fault.
I can't live with him.
I can't live without him.

Terms
by Cassandra Bankson

I am coming to terms with the fact that perhaps I will always
whisper your name
on cold mornings
smile at the passenger seat
before starting the engine
and garner two mugs
when I brew coffee for breakfast
These habits
that hide in the shadow
of routine

"i AM COMING TO TERMS WITH THE FACT THAT PERHAPS i WILL ALWAYS WHISPER YOUR NAME."

– CASSANDRA BANKSON

A Short Page of Fictions
Lucy Ellerton
(Inspired by A Small Fiction by James Miller)

1. "Decision, decision, decision…"
She'd lost them all. Determination, Judgement.
Eight Down could claim no more from her,
Except for the inevitable Conclusion.

2. "Start a conversation."
"But, why?"
"To prove we're real!"
"How do you know we ARE real? Can't I live my life as a figment of imagination?"
"No."
"Why not?"
"Because! Our existence is here, in black and white! You can't view a thought."
"Fine - I'll move to a fictional universe, where my reality makes more sense."
"You can't."
"Why not?"
"She's got writer's block."
"DAMN IT."

3. She looked about the building, drinking in the sight of the beautiful hotel.
"Imagine if these walls could talk, what stories they'd tell…" she sighed as she walked out into the garden.
"Well, if humans would listen, we'd tell her that her husband is cheating on her and he uses this place way too often."
"Oh, and to not use the soap dispenser that last occupant used. That guy was gross."

Chapter Three
Love and Infatuation

Don't Drown
by Eileen Ramos

I don't want this to go further than infatuation. No deeper than surface. Let this remain one-sided and unknown to the object of my desire. I can't risk more without risking losing them and such a loss, I cannot afford.

Not when they could leave my life. I love our conversations too much.

I'm afraid to know them more because they might mar my idealization or worse, become someone I want to give my heart to. This heart has been broken by far less than love and I could only imagine the damage that would befall me if I ever fall out of love.

There's a tall, sweet, southern man I work with that I'm crushing so hard on. He's so kind and always tries to help me but I get confused if he's just being a good co-worker or wants to be my friend. I think it's the former and I never dare to hope for more than friendship. A close friend is pushing me to hit on him but I have a feeling it'd be unrequited. I don't want to make things awkward at work.

Like the saying goes, "don't shit where you eat." And I know of one friend who has to deal with her ex at work and elsewhere and how terrible that is.

But there's a part of me that hopes for more and actually, I dreamed that he stood there in front of me and bent down, while gently lifting my left hand to his lips and letting them caress. I remember how his eyes carefully shut behind his frames and I was touched by his softness. Then in another daring act, he kissed me and I felt my heart burst from mutual tenderness.

"i LOVE OUR
CONVERSATIONS
TOO MUCH."

-EiLEEN RAMOS

I woke up feeling elated and subsequently crestfallen to find that none of it was real. As much as I love that scene, I wish I didn't remember. I wanted to punch my subconscious in the face. I wish I had a nightmare instead. At least afterwards I'd feel relief and consolation, and not this dashed hope that may never come true. I told a friend about this almost-hated dream and he told me that it could still happen.

I want to believe, but I think I'll be pragmatic and just focus on keeping the desire small and insignificant. Maintain its school-girl-crush size. A pleasant distraction not erratic desperation. I have better things to worry about than if he likes me or not. My friendships tend to be more fulfilling than any romantic relationship I've ever established.

I wonder if I'll always hope for infatuation with every attractive person I meet. I wonder if I'll get sick of not knowing love and being under the weight of possibility and denial. When will I ever deserve to say yes to love? When will I ever say yes to myself?

If I know that I'm worthy of loving myself, then why can't I believe that someone could love me back? Why can't I just let myself try, just this once?

Then I remember that sad love songs exist, that people die anyway, that not everyone finds true love, or even lasting happiness. So why chance my heart on one person, no matter how much they brighten my world. Why let them be my center, become my world?

I hope my co-worker proves me wrong. I hope anyone proves me wrong. I hope I throw infatuation aside and let love in.

But I'm not brave enough yet, so for now, let our conversations be flirtless and innocent. Don't get too close to him, and limit the compliments. Don't get to know him more than necessary, ask to hang out outside of work, nor even try to find out if he has a partner or not.

Let it stay infatuation and don't you dare let hope in. Keep it as empty and as light as possible. Don't ask about his dreams, fears, and hopes. What makes him happy. Don't try to make him happy. You already know that he wants to publish a middle-grade novel he's working on and that's dangerous enough. Don't fall for him like you know you will. And as quick as you can, find other people to adore from afar so he won't be the only one, like you hope he is.

And if you ever get close to him, don't you fucking dare show this.

He might fall for you too.
And then you're both done for.

Orange Hallways and Affirmations
by Charity Blaine

We always kissed as we walked through the orange hallway in the mall. It was a weird tradition, but if I forgot, he would remember. I would be chattering away about something silly and he would look over; at first I would be puzzled, and then I would laugh as he kissed me. It was the emptiest section, connecting the Farmer's Market to the rest of the main shopping area. I knew though, that that wasn't love. It was just a cute anecdote, something all relationships have… or at least all of my relationships had had.

I said goodnight to him earlier than usual, and he replied, "Are you gonna come or leave me standing in the cold?"

Sometimes I picked him up on my way to work in the morning. He thought I was angry because lately so many women had been flirting with him, out of the blue.

Then he asked if I was really asleep, and I replied that I couldn't sleep, I was too busy feeling sorry for myself.

It was the truth. I was crying but not because women thought he was handsome. He really was handsome. That was the primary reason I had avoided him for so long. He was much too good looking for my tastes or confidence level - broad shoulders, wide smile and straight white teeth, dark hair, kind eyes, narrow waist, strong legs, and muscled arms. I usually liked more "regular" looking men.

He asked anyway, if that's what was causing me grief - the myriad of girls who batted their eyelashes at him or sent him messages via Facebook, unsolicited.

"No, it's not that", I assured him, "I just feel bad I don't get to see you more often. That, and I don't want to drive in the snow tomorrow." I was familiar with anxiety attacks.

Sometimes they weren't based on anything substantial, more just an accumulation of things over time, often even less than that. I am not sure what I expected him to say, he wasn't weak. Ever. He had grown up in the Middle East where life was tough all the time. He typically saw Canadians as spoiled and so used to easy life that even small problems seem monumental. My previous boyfriend disappeared for anxiety attacks; and the ones before that just got angry or told me to change things I didn't know how to change. I didn't want to share that I was upset anymore.

He texted me, "Focus".

"Focus?" I sent back.

"Yeah, Let me explain."

I waited as the little dots appeared under the text bubble showing that he was writing me something.

And then he wrote out a series of affirmations:

"Don't look around to see if ppl are seeing u/Don't seek approval/keep your eyes always on the prize/you are a lion you are a beast you have the heart of 2000 men/there is no holding back/when you walk in the arena/there is maximum commitment/lions don't hold back/stay calm prepared hands steady/no one has the power to stop you/no one has the strength to hold you/so get the job done/don't look around to see if the others are watching/YOU DON'T NEED IT/YOU WILL BE BETTER WITHOUT IT/No matter how many disappointments you have along the way/Just remain focused/to the finish."

I didn't interrupt the flow of messages once. But finally, he slowed,

"Do you need more?"

I laughed to myself, because it was the sweetest thing I'd ever read.

"No, that's so helpful, thank you. Save more for later. I'll need it again sometime."

"Okay, for later. That's what I say to myself when I look in the mirror."

I sat for a moment and didn't reply. It had never dawned on me that he ever felt weak. He walked with confidence, knew his rights, and stood up for himself. He laughed fearlessly, drove quite recklessly and - so I thought, believed in his strength entirely. In his efforts to encourage me, he revealed his own fears.

"Thank you, so much," I wrote back, and I meant it.

My problem isn't usually what others think of me. So his affirmations didn't entirely ring true, but it didn't matter because at that moment, I realized that he loved me and he believed in me. That he was willing to offer as much cheering on as I needed - and who doesn't feel stronger with someone like that on their side? Love isn't just the cute anecdotes, it's the working through the tough times together, orange hallways and words of affirmation.

"AT THAT MOMENT,
i REALIZED THAT HE
LOVED ME + HE
BELIEVED iN ME...
AND WHO DOESN'T
FEEL STRONGER
WiTH SOMEONE
LiKE THAT ON
THEIR SiDE?"

— CHARITY BLAINE

THE **MOLD** THAT GROWS
ON LEFTOVERS IS *HARMLESS*

UNLESS YOU **EAT**
BREATHE
OR **TOUCH** IT

SO IS **POISON**

SO IS LOVE

harmless - Cassandra Bankson

--

Gunpowder Hearts III
by Kaitlyn Luckow

You make my skin
feel light
as if I were
covered in air
and made of
the radiant souls
I have whispered
on my fingertips
and speak like
wildfire
to make the world
Beautiful
again.

Introvert Seeks Introvert
by Meg Colt

Despite my best efforts,
small talk siphons
the energy out of me,
it's nearly painful
in execution.

If you want any chance
at a connection,
give me the real words,
tell me the meaningful things.

I want to hear about
the most vivid dream
you've ever had.

What scared you as a child?

What song that fills your
heart and lungs?

Forget the weather,
don't dare mention the news,
tell me what really matters.

Rain
by Cassandra Bankson

Weather permitting,
might I lean on your shoulder,
memorize the ridges of your back,
rest in the valley of your elbow?
Trace the trails of your heart,
to a pond as deep as the ocean,
swing from the branches of your thoughts
alongside the basketed acorns,
leave my tiny prints
impressed in the softness of your dusty skin?
Cordillera,
The forecast calls for rain.

a letter: dear dad, happy birthday
by Erin Kim

my old hotmail email notified me that it's your birthday. otherwise i think i may have forgotten.

i wonder what you look like now. it's been...i guess 4 years since mom, brother and i decided to run away from you.

when i think about that last memory of seeing you, i don't know how to feel. i remember the background noise of our suitcase's wheels against the parking garage concrete. i remember you shouting at us as you grabbed my arm and i was scared and without thinking, i pushed you off me. i don't remember what you said. i just remember the rush and the sharp noises. and i remember that even though i knew it was right to leave you, i also knew that you loved me. that's what confuses me.

even though we left you, i continued to feel your presence in the dark trauma that you left in mom's head and heart and bones. i was reminded of you by her deep, dark, cavernous depression that seemed to have no end.

but as she has been moving forward, i have been trying to understand who you are to me. although i never emotionally felt connected to you - like i could be truly vulnerable and share myself with you - i always knew that you loved me. i always did, and i do feel that you believe in me. i'm not sure if i knew this by the presents you diligently brought me back from all your international mysterious business trips, or by our trips to eat the best korean bbq on special occasions, or if it's by how you spoiled me with travels to paris, austria, quebec and other cities all before i was fifteen.

"i FEEL THAT i
HAVE TO SAY SORRY,
THOUGH i DON'T
BELIEVE i'VE DONE
ANYTHING WRONG."
— ERIN KIM

i'm not sure how i'm sure of your love, but i know that despite how you may have broken us with your addiction to the game, to money, to the wry hope in gambling, i couldn't be who i am today without you. and i know you love me. and i believe, i know, i love you.

so i take a moment on your special day, to reflect a little more deliberately about you when usually i give most of my daily joy and energy in celebrating mom in a way that you did not.

today, i hope you are eating more than just cup ramen. this year, i hope you don't have to beg for loans anymore. i hope you don't have to play games anymore. i hope you can find peace in yourself, solace in a new way of life, hope and respect in this world, if not in god.

i feel that i have to say sorry, though i don't believe i've done anything wrong. i wish i could help you. i don't know what you need right now. but i can say, from the bottom of my heart, i wish you the happiest day, and i love you dad.

[i share this tonight in part because i don't know many peers with gambling fathers. in case you have one like so, you are not alone. and he is not alone either.

we belong to our families in unique ways.]

From: Erin Kim
Sent: Today 12:52 AM
To: dad
Subject: happy birthday!

hi dad!

happy birthday to you! how are you doing?

here are some photos of me. one of them is from halloween - i dressed in my own victorian punk style. i even won a costume contest!

in another photo, i am at the opening of another art show my photos are a part of. i am eating a snack in my mouth. in the last photo, i am selling small stories/mini paper magazines at an arts and craft fair in nyc. all those things on the desk are small books/art pieces i have made.

this summer i even got to do a talk to an audience - i talked about self empowerment to maybe 150 people.

i know you mentioned last time that you loved to see my art – if you're ok with it, i would be happy to mail you some of my small art prints so you can see it yourself!

i wish you'll have a great birthday and year moving forward. i hope you are eating healthy and exercising. i remember you would often go to the gym and take good care of your body. i have just started to go to the gym near my work, and i hope i get stronger too.

god bless you dad.

-erin

From: dad
Sent: Monday, July 24, 2017 1:03 AM
To: Erin Kim
Subject: Re: art show

에린이가 이렇게 훌륭한 작품을 만들줄은 아빠는생각도 못했지.

이제는 완전히 profesional artist가 됐군아. 무엇보다도 에린이가 좋아하는 일을 하니까 아빠는 기분이 좋아.

사진을 보니까 에린이가 더 세련되고 이뻐진 거 같은데.

translation: i never would've guessed you would made such wonderful art work.

i see you're now officially a professional artist. more than anything, i'm happy to see you doing something that makes you happy.

judging from the photos, i think you've gotten more sophisticated and pretty.

이제부터 에린이가 생각날 때 마다 아빠는 에린이가 보낸 이 작품들을 볼거야.

아빠는 항상 에린이가 자랑스러워. 모든지 열심히 하니까...

now, whenever i think of you, i will look at your art you've shown me here.

i'm always proud of you, erin. because you always give your best.

에린이 피곤할 때 발 마사지를 못해주니까 안타깝네.

에린이가 잘 먹고 건강하기를 항상 기도하지.

i feel bad that i cannot give you a foot massage when you are tired

(erin speaking: i promise this is not that weird if it sounds weird)

i'm always praying that you will eat well and stay healthy.

에린이 작품 보내줘서 고마워.

thank you for sharing your art works with me.

i love Erin a lot !!!
-dad

i'm a reply, a text, a DM, a vibe away.
-erin

Gunpowder Hearts IV
by Kaitlyn Luckow

You taste like
smoke and mirrors
riddled with the notion
that my skin
can look inside
and be without
as I cease to crumble
and choose to
whisper in the wind instead

A Bird's Song
by Rhianna Lesik

He said that
the birds
have far too much
to talk about,
and this is why they
sing.

The storytelling
starts early,
they share secrets
among the wind;
only to have their hymn
follow my tracks back home.

- I wonder what they say about us

Hand in Hand
by Haley Littlefield

You have searched my soul.
You have stood at the forks in my veins and wondered which
way was correct.
With every doubt trying to pull us apart, you have turned the
corners of my being until you found light.
And I ask again and again,
Why do you love me?
Panic is my middle name.
Tears are constantly streaming down my face.
My skin is bubbling with stress.
I feel like my veins are trying to escape my body,
Like my blood is flies, buzzing up and down my limbs,
Like my heart wants to leap out of my chest with you holding on
for dear life,
Like my lungs are clenched tight and low, waiting to pounce.
My own organs want to leave me.

And I just want to hold you,
But I'm afraid of what might happen.
I'd love for you to catch some of this fire,
But I am worried you might put me out.
I'm begging you, don't go.
Please, I need you,
But don't be surprised,
When I ask you why you've chosen to stay.

And yet, my love,
You never leave.
Together, we have run forward,
And we have backtracked.
We have gotten so lost.
We have left things behind.
We have been distracted.
We have been awestruck.

We have been scared to go on,
But we have always found our way back home.
You have held me when I am nothing but embers burning your eyes,
And even though it hurts sometimes,
We have done it all,
Hand in hand.

" i JUST WANT
TO HOLD YOU
BUT iM
AFRAID OF
WHAT MiGHT
HAPPEN."

– HALEY LITTLEFIELD

Indescribable
by Haley Littlefield

"What is it like to fall for someone? Like, really fall?" he said.

She looks up and smiles. She says, "Okay, are you ever just minding your own business at night when suddenly, you see the moon and you feel ever so slightly breathless, like you pause your life for a second because holy wow, it's so big and bright. Surely, it isn't always that big and bright. Or you know how sometimes the sun shines through the cracks in your blinds and it's like you can suddenly see the air? It creates little beams of light, glistening, and making dust look like stars in your living room.

Okay, that's what falling in love is like. Suddenly seeing things all around you in a different way.

No, it's more than that. It's like you're thinking about them without thinking about them because they are consuming you brain like some kind of sexy zombie. You have no choice in the matter. Okay, but it's more than that... it's more than a crazy obsession. It's like you know they are not perfect and you love them anyway. Only they are perfect. Perfectly imperfect. Your one and only. Shit like that. Yes, it's actually all of the cliches you can think of and more.

Did your grandma ever buy you a doll for Christmas that was the most beautiful doll you ever saw, but you weren't supposed to play with it because it was "a collectible" and you understood and placed her gently on a shelf - but, when some time passed and you just knew that Victorian winter barbie would look amazing in your Britney Spears doll's sassy schoolgirl outfit? You just knew. So, you give in and tear her clothes off and it is amazing and, now you feel kind of sick and awful yet, powerful and free at the same time. It's like that.

It's when someone gently touches your skin in just the right way and every hair on your body stands up, reaching out, begging for more. You are in this vulnerable ecstasy and you like it. But it's also the other side of it. It's that second where you stop and revel in the power you could have over another person. And then you give them more.

Oh, I know. It's like reading your favorite book for the first time... You didn't know when you picked it up. You might have had a inkling about it, but you didn't know. You liked the cover... You knew the premise... Sure, he's a great author, but you didn't know. With each page turn you fall further and further into a world where you belong; where someone gets you, where everything is romantic in the philosophical sense of the word and the closer you get to the end, the less you want to read because you don't want it to be over - but you have to keep going because you need the closure and you've never felt so powerless even though it's just a book and you probably need to chill a little bit. You pull it close to you and hug it. Metaphorically, I mean. It's like an indescribable feeling, but you know it exactly. I know you do.

Okay, maybe it's simply like laying down on the world's most comfortable bed. And you're very sleepy. You get all snuggled in and someone says, "You can have it. It's yours. Congratulations, you get to sleep on a cloud forever." It's like being wrapped up and feeling calm and safe in a way you've never felt in your whole life. It's home.

Well, darling, there's nothing like it."

Old Habits – Bounce Back
by Rhea Smith

Love is
I don't know what
to say, that
it hurts, it stings,
it makes me rage
and all of the pain
people have inflicted
the memories of what
could have been, should have been
I keep wondering, what
I did to deserve that?
Is there anything
I should change?
I know it's not healthy to think that
But then I bounce right back.

Chapter Four
Everyday Life

"SO STOP.
AND SOAK IN
THE COLORS OF
THE STILL AND
PAINT YOUR
SKIN IN
THE NOW."

-KAITLYN LUCKOW

Midnight Blooms III
by Kaitlyn Luckow

Time blurs forward
whether you walk
or run.
      So stop.
and soak in
the colors of
the still and
paint your skin
in the now.

Punch.
by Suzanna Valentine Moore

I always wondered what would qualify me to be a
Card Carrying Adult.

What would that day look like? Would I be ready?

But then I realized, it's not one day.
One moment.

The proverbial Card is more like a punch card that you just
fill up as you get older.

But they get more complicated as you get older, too.

Making your bed voluntarily.
PUNCH.

Eating nutritious meals all day (or just once?)
PUNCH.

Paying your bills on time.
PUNCH.

Taking your meds or vitamins or birth control.
PUNCH.

Buying a bra that actually fits you.
PUNCH.

Putting someone else's needs in front of your own.
PUNCH

Sometimes, though, they seem less like minor victories and
more like punches in the face.

Your house getting broken into.
PUNCH.

Someone harassing you at a bar.
PUNCH.

Cutting someone out of your life, even if you love them.
PUNCH.

Attending a loved one's funeral.
PUNCH.

Putting your needs in front of someone else's.
PUNCH.

Nourishment
by Cassandra Bankson

Eating is the hardest part
The daunting fear of falling apart
When giving in
You're letting go
Accepting the fear
A trade for control
Releasing the mask
Relapse to addiction
You can only be beat
By your own decisions
To spill your guts
And flip a table
Still tethered to
An emotional cable
Vomiting words
And spilling dreams
Coming undone
By your body's own seams
When bad decisions
Land upon your feet
The stench of remorse
Is no longer so sweet
Isolation inviting
Reflection rejecting
Some mental disorders
Make mouths unaccepting.

Everyday Life
by Charity Blaine

Those people who show you beauty where you wouldn't look -
Who share small meaningful moments as a collage of their lives -
Have done this as a shield against a bigger sadness they are fighting.

You see an ideal life and sometimes might be jealous of it -
But the reality is they are in a personal war and those moments
are their bombs. The world is sometimes too heavy,
so they look for small victories
In everyday life -
And it becomes Art.

Every Day
by Caz Brett

It arrives. Steady, a dulcet rumbling as it clamours towards me; it brings with it the inflecting squeal of the brakes and scraping of steel on steel. My slow eyes raise to greet it reluctantly and I stare vacantly at the air between us.

There is movement to either side of me, but there is no need to turn around. I am surrounded by clones. They never acknowledge their kind, and I am one of them. I am invisible. My briefcase matches theirs, not in style but in substance - or the lack of - that it contains. Documents that seem important but are meaningless and exist only to justify my existence. Our existence. Us, the invisible clone army. Soundlessly, we edge in line towards the worn lines of the platform, being careful to place ourselves on either side of every dirty mark.

As it comes to a final stop, my eyes begin to focus. My brain whirrs into action as I take it off standby in preparation for the battle ahead. I am looking at hands and faces pressed up against the glass, but I am unseeing. There is always a space that can be made. We are a class of magicians creating matter from nothing. Here, today, physics is thrown out of the window.

The familiar hiss of the doors sounds as they release and swing open towards us. We stand together, alert but still dormant. There is perhaps a lull of one second, one very long and breathless second as we all pause, before the waves begin tumbling towards us. The attack begins.

I hold steady. My arms are slightly wider than my body, a shield to deflect away that onslaught of arms and umbrellas and briefcases. A surge sends me stumbling to one side, but one swift elbow later and I've edged back into position. The first wave slows, and I spy newer and greedier clones pushing forwards. I frown towards them but their eyes are on the prize;

70

they think they have won and I see an expression of smug elation spread across their faces as they edge just in front. They think they have somehow beaten the game; that they've flouted the agreed social rules and got ahead. The rest of us know better, but we say nothing. This is their lesson to learn.

We watch with well-practised apathy. As they briskly step up towards the bright lights of home, they are caught off guard by a sudden, violent vomit of colours, of angry voices, of frustration. They are in the wrong place, the wrong time, and the stream is too strong; in that instant we see their faces spasm - in just one cruel moment, they are lost, dragged away with the undercurrent. The stream of people carries them away. We have already forgotten about them.

Those of us who remain stagger back and brace for this second wave. It spews forth from all edges of the doors, pouring ceaselessly onto the platform and bringing another deluge; this time, sharpened elbows and backpacks and psychological trauma. I am prepared. I grit my teeth as the brunt of the crowd hits me again, but this time, I squeeze through and travel upstream. I am besieged, beset by the hot pounding of blood in my ears and the invisible pressing barrier of societal expectation bearing down on every side. It wears away at my very core, making me question all that I am and all that I can be. I navigate the flow of people, advancing further towards the doors. I negotiate the step with care, and I throw myself into the safety of bodies - fellow clones - who do not greet me but instead begrudgingly accept that I, too, have been successful.

They politely move their sensible leather brogues to one side as I slot mine into a gap four times smaller than my foot. It isn't over yet, and we all know it. We are now permitted to silently recoup our breaths and cram our bodily attributes into every crevasse we can. We nudge uncomfortably forwards, and wait. We wait.

I have slotted into the grey area, the middle ground. This is still a combat zone. I am paused, slick with anticipation and flush with anxiousness, contorting my head until it falls into the safe space; behind the amnesty of the doors. I rest my ear on the woollen jacket of the gentlemen to my right, and a loose strand scrapes my lobe. I am paralysed, my hand trapped between my case and the clones compressed together in front of me, and I cannot pull myself away. I must endure.

My thoughts are disturbed by the disingenuous high-pitched serenade of the doors closing, and collectively, we hold our breath. The swooshing arms of the rubber folds rush to greet us - but there is a problem. My ears begin to bleed to the sound of a violent banshee scream as the doors are alert to an obstruction. The doors cannot close behind us. We can magic the space, but even this compression of matter has its limit.

Silent accusatory glares flow across the carriage as silent and awkward, we stand. In the grey area, we renegotiate our territories, standing firm but shuffling our legs, intertwining them to find the room we need. But it is not enough. Once again the rubber edges rush towards a passionate embrace only to find themselves unable to fulfill their partnership, and like before they are wrenched apart with a scream. This is it. This is the final stand.

We are vicious. Acting as one, we hone in on the weakest. We smell their fear. We can detect an aura of compassion, a predilection for empathy, and we reach out towards it with our minds. We salivate heartlessness and we are truculent, unstopping, as we bend ourselves towards them, collectively gathering invisibly the matter we have materialised and we shuffle, each millimetre shift of an elbow weakening their defences. We absorb matter, we inflate and take up just a little more space, we loosen our bodies so they are less tightly compact and we all watch with beady eyes as the sweat dribbles down the neck of the person in front.

72

The ground is shrinking beneath his feet and the shoes suddenly don't fit the space he has tentatively claimed. Shaky, we can sense him dithering, the clockwork cogs in his head chugging into overdrive. He knows the cost of the battle must be him but he still fights.

How intolerably human of him. How frustrating.

And like that, he jumps. The platform feels a million miles away now and we can see him landed there. We ooze into the space he's left behind and soak it in. It's like he was never there.

Wordlessly victorious, we watch him out of the corners of our eyes as the rubber lips rush towards each other like long-lost lovers and this time they are tightly caressing, holding each other until the next stop will tear them apart once more. Sealed inside, the clones hold their positions as the engine jerks into action and cries its way out of the station, straight into the endless black tunnel ahead.

"HOW
INTOLERABLY
HUMAN..."
  —CAZ BRETT

Untitled III
by Cassandra Bankson

The excitement
the thrill
the rush
the laughter
The kind of adventure every soul is after.
A car
canned food
open roads
and sharp bends
An endless adventure
of two lifelong friends.
State lines
county borders
new houses
old rafters
Picking a place
to live happily ever after.

Midnight Blooms IV
by Kaitlyn Luckow

Through the fields
of sun
I saw the shadow beneath
and knew
it wouldn't
be covered for long.
so I created
my own
and asked the rays
to dance.

We Can Learn From Nature
by Cassandra Bankson

Rose petals, butterfly wings
Beauty that hangs by delicate hinges.
Like the amber fingerprints of birch trees
(who shed leaves from their twisted knuckles)
We let go of those who no longer refresh our souls
So that we are able to transform.
Create room to sow love
In the gardens of our hearts.

Through the chaos of the seasons
Find serenity in the metamorphosis.
Stable as the steadfast trunks of trees
Systematic as the puzzle pieces of their bark
And even through death and decay
They leave the benevolent gift of life.
Carpets of mulch give way to a cluster of toxic shroom,
Young velvet clover knowing not from which they come
Abundance flourishing from the grave
Creating quilted mosaics of moss
That lean into the spontaneous drops of rain.

The forest dances barefoot
To choreographed light and shadow
Spinning like the currents
Who kiss and caress the stones of the riverbed
Flowing with intention,
bubbling with life.

Chapter Five
Everything Else

To The Man Sitting Across From Me In The Subway
by Erin Kim

New York

It was 10pm. A Saturday in June. I'd just gotten on the A (or maybe it was the C) headed uptown at the West 4th street station. The train was quiet. There weren't very many people aboard. I was wearing a white collared linen dress, tan Oxford shoes, my black hair was done up, and I carried a black purse and some pastries in a white plastic bag that read "Panya." You were sitting across from me. You wore a blue and white vertical-striped button down shirt, khaki pants, and brown boat shoes. You had a gray watch on your left wrist, and more interestingly a bright pink neon band on the right wrist; the black text on it said "UNICORN". You were hunching forward, elbows resting on your thighs.

A minute into the subway ride, I realized you were looking at me. Your gaze was too deep to have been a happenstance moment of our eyes randomly meeting. You must've been looking at me since I sat down. In that brief glance I realized how handsome you were–you had short dark hair, you wore form-fitting clothes, you had no facial hair. I was nervous, smitten, that you'd notice me, but I was glad because it was a day I had dressed up, so I knew I didn't look too bad.

Out of nervousness, I looked off to my right, at the train window as tunnel lights flashed by. I could feel your steady gaze on me from my peripheral vision, but I wasn't brave enough to meet your eyes again. For that, I'm sorry. Every time you looked away, I stole the moment to take a glance at you, and confirm my hunch that you were in fact handsome and adorable. But when you looked at me again, I looked away. In the moment, I tried to convince myself you were not staring at me, but I'm quite sure you were; I wouldn't have been so nervous otherwise. I played with the jewelry and rings on my fingers to keep me busy as the train moved slowly onward. You checked your phone for a bit. So did I. I had my white spaghetti-string headphones in, but no music was playing; I was listening to a slow soundtrack of silence, hearing every second go by as a missed opportunity to say something to you.

At 34th street Penn Station, a man stepped in asking "This goin' downtown?" You said, "Going uptown." Hearing your voice was lovely. You sounded exactly like I would've imagined. You seemed immediately sweet, without being overly saccharine.

As we reached the 42nd street Port Authority station, you and I both started to fix our positions to leave. I was excited to notice you were getting off at the same stop. I left the train first, and started to walk up the steps, hoping that maybe I'd still be walking with you when we left the station. I made it through the crowd of people rushing down to catch the train that was still there. At the top of the steps, I turned around. I saw that you went back on the train; you were sitting down again. You moved to the train car next to "ours."

I was so confused; why did you change cars? Did you realize it wasn't your stop? You were ready to get off the station well before the train conductor announced the stop…You should've known what stop it was. Did you get off at the station just to try to catch me, but then somehow changed your mind as I walked up the steps? Did you just hate that one train car, so you wanted a change in scenery? I like to think that you were considering leaving with me; I was sad to see you go.

The train doors were still open. I even considered running down the steps to get back onto that train. I hesitated for a few good seconds as the car doors hesitated to close; they beeped a few times as if they'd shut, but they didn't, as if they were giving me a last chance to make a move. But I figured, as I saw you sat down, my chance was over. So I continued on my way.

I would've loved to start a conversation with you, to ask you, "Is this train going uptown?" just to hear more of your voice. I wish I held your gaze. I wish I smiled when you looked at me. I wish I said "hello." I wonder what we'd talk about. I wonder what you're like. I don't doubt you're sweet; how could I be so sure? I don't know, yet I feel that I know. And I feel right about that.

I've never enjoyed glancing at someone on public transportation before. I've never regretted not saying something to someone like this ever before, so I write about it even a few days after the event. I keep looking for you in crowds and in the streets of New York, as if I'd find you magically in front of my eyes like you happened to be sitting in front of me that Saturday evening. Maybe you'll see this. Maybe you feel the same way. Maybe I'll see you again, on the A, or maybe it was the C, going uptown.

Summit
by Cassandra Bankson

They say
It is difficult to reach the pinnacle of a mountain
Dangerous even
If you are not well planned and prepared
But I am not afraid
For heights and depths
Appear flat
After conquering you

Echo
by Rebecca Foley
Illustrated by Chelsea Lewis

I walk quickly, trying to avoid eye contact with her. Maybe she won't notice me today. "Hey, Axel!" she calls snidely.

Closing my eyes, I let out a large sigh and turn towards her,

"What do you want this time, Lexa?"

"I just wanted to give you some advice."

"And what would that be?" I ask, not missing a beat.

"First off, maybe you should put a bag over your head. You're going to cause someone to go blind one of these days. I'm sure you already have, though. I don't want to be one of those people so could you just cover your face already?" I just stand there, avoiding eye contact. "You're ugly, short, and fat. You're the biggest idiot I know. You are worthless!"

I shake my head as a tear rolls down my cheek. "You may think I'm all those things," I say to her, "but I know I'm not. And even if I am, I'm proud of who I am. I may be short and I may not look like the models in a magazine but damn do I look good. My skin is my skin and you know what it's the best damn skin I could ask for. I may make dumb mistakes every once in awhile, but I'm smarter than I was yesterday and I'll continue to become smarter through my mistakes. I am not worthless. I am me!"

A great sigh of relief is released from my body. She has put me down every day for years and today I accept and love who I am no matter what anyone else says. I take one last look at

Lexa and walk away from the mirror, ready to take on the world with my new-found confidence.

Wash Our Hands III
by Kaitlyn Luckow

Rays speckle their
way into the cracks
of shadows
and the petals
still arise
through the rain.

Tomorrow isn't promised
But we make plans anyways.

Psych Unit
by Cassandra Bankson

It's the familiar aroma of antiseptic cleansers and latex handshakes.

Not the kind of handshakes that welcome you to your overpriced Tahitian resort for the next week, but the kind that feel more like seismic shakes. A firm grip around a fragile wrist to control a flailing limb, the tremors of cardiac line on its electronic monitor, the frantic rattling of a gurney's clingy wheels as its gussied through a maze of corridors it knows all too well.

Here, fluorescent bulbs line sterile halls and wash away any perception of night and day.

If you squint your eyes, the speckled linoleum tiles look identical to the floaters that cloud your morning vision if you try to stand up too quickly.

This is the kind of place where dizzy thoughts meet sedating prescriptions, as benzodiazepines make their home in strangers' veins.

It is here, among countless names and numbers that I've spent the majority of the last two months.

Residency within these soundproof walls feels like anything but home. The white coats you're obliged to wear are a far cry from the Friday night styles you'd expect to see in downtown Manhattan. The professionalism of stern roommates is so sterile, you'd wonder if they still know how to converse outside of patient charts.

There are no family dinners or roaring game nights here, and when the phone rings, it's rarely a relative with good news.

If you take a moment to ease your hunchback and lift your lethargic gaze from a clipboard or abstract art of an x ray, you'll notice the subtleties that aren't portrayed on prime time's evening forensic shows.

The unspoken language of faces that convey a lack of hope or interest, the mental clockwork of doctoral genius that operate against hands of time, the countless bleached blankets, food trays and socks that are recycled and reused like prescription papers and donors' parts.

Tonight's episode isn't one that you can find on-demand, and isn't one that most would want to watch, let alone play a role in.

As antipsychotics wage war on my perception, the back of my tongue savors the metallic taste of this rigid hospital bed without ever escaping my lips.

The medical codes bubble out of nurses mouths the way biohazardous fluids do from jaundiced skin, but none of the ambient sounds seem to make sense, other than the lullaby of screeching elevator doors.

As blurry as the walls, faces, and lines that divide reality from delusions are, it's admirable to realize how calculated each of these blue and white pawns are to this traumatic game of chess.

A game in which I am the queen, and my army of chemical rooks, bishops and knights ride gallant horses of IV tubes and needles to keep me safe.

Even when I attempt to weave the nurses' stories about my Ivy League education, experience in the post op unit downstairs, and the achievement of front row parking earlier this week, each of my words are discredited as manic garble;

thrown aside carelessly the way a mistress does her dress, or a cancer patient does their meal.

A salad of inaudible words, reduced to a line of static is all that actually makes its way out from behind my teeth. A complete distortion of the thoughts that are so elegantly strung together between my ears.

Regardless of my momentary identity as a student, world famous musician, exalted messiah, or Spartan messenger, the only respect I'm given comes in the form of leather "strap-you-to-the-gurney-for-your-own-protection" jewelry and a peppery white gown.

In society and psych wards alike, nobody wants to believe you unless you wield the shield of a medical badge or illusion of suburban upper class, bleached collar existence.

Similar veils of cotton reality cover other lifeless, or sleeping patients; the sardined bodies and their salt stained faces that over the next three months will become the kind of friends you don't want to keep in touch with.

When skin and speech are no longer erupting like an active volcano and your strength is finally contained by restraints and prescriptions, you are given a crystal palace to build a fortress in for the next three days of September; year 5150, or whatever era your mind decides to make of it.

You are free to orbit the bed they expect you to sleep on, and like a figure skater competing for gold, they watch and analyze you through glass and screens, both thick enough that you wouldn't be able to break.

The unit is a place similar to nothing other than birth and death itself. Upon arrival you are stripped of everything you own and expected to survive with minimal guidance. When your time has eclipsed, you leave with nothing but a release paper and a limp white sheet they have the audacity to call a gown.

Sleepwalkers
by Rhea Smith

I am incredibly uncomfortable.

I don't know why I thought today of all days was the one to bring my gym bag as well as my backpack to class, especially knowing it was going to rain. I stumbled into the classroom, late as usual, and didn't look a single person in the eye. Furthest row to the left, six seats back. I set down my backpack, gym bag, overcoat, sweatshirt, gloves, hat, and scarf on the desk behind me—no one ever sat there. Not sure if it's because of me, or because it's such an isolated part of the room, and I don't really care to know either.

"Wie geht's?"

I looked up—my teacher was standing near my desk, and I finally took a moment to look around. Everyone else had their textbook out, working quietly on a writing prompt, and I had only just sat down. I mumbled a humble "nichts, bin gut" and quickly dug into my backpack for the textbook.

Before I could open my mouth to ask, my teacher answered my question. 'Drei und zwanzig'. I nod, just barely thanking her loud enough for her to catch it, and flip to page 23. Just as I get to that page, my finger slides down the fibers of the sheet and slits right down the middle. I gasp, but it doesn't hurt. A paper cut that didn't hurt. Bizarre. Not really, I guess. Nerve endings only go so far, right?

"Warum bist du… late again?" I hear from next to me. Warren is whispering at me. Warren is the only person who will actually speak to me in this class, and I'm grateful for it—but my incessant need to look cool will never let me admit that to "i AM INCREDIBLY UNCOMFORTABLE."

– RHEA SMITH

him. I shrugged, and he laughed at me. "By the way… St. Patrick's Day," he said. I looked down, and sighed.

Shit.

He reached over, grabbed my arm, and pinched.

It's cold. Cold enough that I can see my own breath. I frantically turn a couple circles, looking for any of the belongings I had come with. When did I even start standing up? Nothing. What I wouldn't give for those gloves and scarf right now, let alone the sweater and coat.

What really ought to have been my main focus right now, though, just about slapped me silly with reality. Or rather—and that's just it—the lack thereof. I wasn't in the classroom any longer.

In fact, I wasn't even sure I was in San Francisco any longer. None of my surroundings made any sense. I had the sensation of being in a forest, or some kind of deep nature setting, but I couldn't distinguish any trees around me. It wasn't for a lack of lighting—though it were dim, it wasn't dark enough for me to be blind to my surroundings. It was more peculiar than that—it was as if I were in the background of an oil painting, where the trees were too small to be defined as anything more than smudges on a canvas.

Shivers ran down my spine and I knew I wasn't alone. I turned a few paces again—maybe a full circle? Everything blended together, I couldn't tell my left from my right. Fingers encircled my wrist, and suddenly all of the smudges were being pulled violently to the right. Or rather, I was being pulled to the left.

I looked down to observe my captor, only to realize I was at eye level with a young girl. Am I dreaming of Alice in Wonderland? When the tree-smudges finally stopped moving, we were in total darkness. I think. I couldn't tell, because everything around us was black as could be, but the girl herself was so brightly lit.

"Alara," she said, as if answering the question I had not yet thought—who is she? Before that thought could register was when I saw the first one. The first sleepwalker. And at that moment, I was running. Or at least, trying to. The sleepwalker appeared to be getting smaller, but the black around me was motionless—for obvious reasons. All the same, Alara had not moved a single inch, as if we were both standing still in the same room. She gave me the most peculiar look.

"Where are you going? You just got back, after all this time," she said, crossing her arms. Something about her face looked so familiar. I shook my head.

"What do you mean? I've never seen you before," I said. Because that was the obvious thing to ask the only person who appears to know what's going on in a place where those things are walking around rampant. Her eyes widened.

"How long were you in there for? I know it was a few days, but good grief Sama, you'd think you'd lived…" she started, and then stopped mid-sentence as if she had realized something.

"Excuse my language, but what the fuck are you talking about?"

"Here."

Her fingers encircled my wrist once more, and again I had the sensation of moving—but I wasn't even moving my feet. Suddenly, I was surrounded by hundreds, maybe thousands of them. My heart was pounding in my chest, reminiscent of the kind of fear one should have at seeing something like that. Adrenaline pulsed through my veins and suddenly, I could see them.

They were like people. Sort of.

Very blurry people.

She pulled me closer to the nearest one—a short one—and guided my hand towards its face. I pulled away before I could touch it.

"What the hell are you- what is- what the fuck?" I asked, holding my hand to my chest. She sighed.

"You really were in there for a whole lifetime, weren't you?"

I closed my eyes. This makes no sense. None of this makes sense. I'm dreaming. This is a nightmare. I reached down to my leg, pressed my fingers against my flesh, and pinched. Immediately, I heard a giggle. I opened my eyes—nothing had changed.

"You can't come out of a dream if you're not in one, you goof," she said, in a sing-song voice, "now touch the damn girl."

How could she even tell it was a girl? These creatures were so blurred, there's no way—I finally looked back at the 'creature' to see a toddler, eyes closed, slightly rocking back and forth as if sleeping standing up.

"I just...?" I said, reaching my hand out to the toddler's face. Alara nodded. My fingers made contact with the tiny girl's temples.

"Meems, let's go!" cried out Avery. I opened my eyes. Everything had changed again. But something in my chest had lifted—I felt elated. A feeling you can only really truly feel as a toddler exploring the word for the first time. A boy, whom I somehow knew as Avery, was holding out his hand. I had butterflies in my stomach—a childhood crush? He took my hand, and we walked down the steps of his basement.

"Remember, we can't tell anybody," he said, and he led me around the banister and to a padlocked door under the staircase. He tugged at it, and it sprung open. "It's been broken for weeks, but no one noticed."

The door swung open, and there was a box laying amongst a bunch of bags of old clothing and winter wear. Avery knelt down and pulled the box toward him—suddenly, I had a sinking feeling in the pit of my stomach. The elated feeling was completely gone, and I somehow knew what was going to happen next—as if this were a dream of something that had happened before…

"No," I said, urging Avery to put it back. He ignored me, didn't even acknowledge my words. I had no control over this. He pulled the lid from the box and exposed a rifle. "Cool," I could hear myself say, and yet my brain was screaming 'run'.

"Right? My daddy never keeps it loaded so I like to pretend I'm him at the range, or like I'm one of those actors in those movies my mommy doesn't know he lets me watch," Avery said, and lifted the gun out of the box. I remember this. I know where this is going. I don't want to. I can't watch this. He held the gun out towards me, and I took the cold handle into my hand.

"No!" I managed, finally able to take control of my body, and I reached down to pinch my thigh.

All at once, I was wrenched right back to the dark place. Alara stood there, eyebrows raised.

"Sorry about that. I forgot this one killed her friend, she has nightmares about it pretty often. That's my bad," Alara said, completely unfazed.

"My bad?" I asked, "My bad?! I almost shot a little boy and that's all you have to say?"

"You didn't shoot him. That boy is already dead. Meems shot him. I think... two months ago? It's hard to judge time when dreams move so quickly," Alara said, pacing but not moving in space. I closed my eyes, took a deep breath, and finally decided to take the plunge.

"What is this? Who are you?" I asked.

"Oh Sama. It's not who am I, it's who are we. We're the others. We watch the sleepwalkers. Make sure they don't get hurt, you know?"

I looked around. Suddenly, the silhouettes looked a little more sharpened. The hundreds, thousands—they were all asleep.

"I'm not. I'm human. I'm... Then how come I have all these memories? I was just in German class, and Warren..." I said, and suddenly I realized how quickly those memories were fading—as if waking up from a dream. My breath caught in my chest.

"You were in her dream. For a really long time, actually. You shouldn't do that, you know that. They don't like it when you take over for too long," Sama said, and gestured towards a silhouette that was shaking violently.

"That's... me?" I asked, stepping closer. She looked exactly like me.

"No, that's the sleepwalker you touched days ago and didn't leave until just a few moments ago," she sighed. I could hear the lack of patience in her voice.

"Well, how do I get back? That was my life," I said, reaching out to touch her. Alara grabbed my wrist, stopping me.

"You can't go back. Don't you realize? She has a mind of her own. When you step into their mind, you take over, but they're still there. She's shaking because she's angry. You were there when she was awake, you were only supposed to make sure she was safe when she was sleeping, Sama. You fucked up."

"She's angry?" I asked, pulling my hand away. I stared at my—her, rather—body. It kept shaking violently, thrashing to the right and left, occasionally disappearing from sight. Alara nodded.

"Just leave her alone."

"But I have to go back."

"No. You can't go back. We never touch the same dreamer in the same cycle. You shouldn't have been in her mind for as long as you did. I'm serious Sama, you fucked up."

"So what, I'm just stuck here?" I yelled. Alara looked at me, dumbstruck.

"What the fuck do you mean stuck here? This is us. This is what we do. You have so many dreamscapes you can touch, just pick one and go," she said, crossing her arms. "You just can't go back to that one. Remember, you're not her. She's not you. You were just a passenger."

This can't be real. I'm fucking dreaming. I pinched myself again, harder than ever.

99

Nothing happened.

Wash Our Hands IV
by Kaitlyn Luckow

All of our scars align
and we had
our palms up
for everyone to see
to illuminate our destruction
and how it let us
become anew.
Because we're all heading
in the same direction
and in it, we are
the same.

About the Authors and Artists

Cassandra Bankson

When we lose ourselves in books, we often find pieces of ourselves that we forgot existed. Cassandra Bankson didn't always identify herself as a writer, although she did identify writing as healing. Certain parts of life, love and emotion can't be expressed through language alone, but are easily woven into poems like threads of cotton or silk that clothe our minds and keep our hearts warm. Cassandra finds expression in different mediums: she has been a YouTube Video Creator and Blogger since 2010, focusing on igniting conversations surrounding how we perceive beauty, define it, and express it. She channels these messages through creative makeup tutorials, skincare based science posts, and motivational "sitting on the living room floor" conversations. She is currently studying with a trajectory of Dermatology and Psychology, hoping to change the way the medical system treats our skin, bodies, and emotions; including the way we treat and perceive ourselves on a day to day basis. Cassandra is a firm believer that knowledge is power, and she hopes that by sharing her experiences and inviting opportunity for difficult conversations to take place, others can learn, grow from, and find solace within those spaces. It is her life mission to help others live beautifully, both inside and out.

Caz Brett

Caz Brett has always been surprised that the men in white coats did not take her away when she wrote a short poem about dead pigs when she was 5. She is a feminist and all-round creative person from London, and writes short stories and personal pieces, often covering subjects like depression and anxiety. She enjoys avoiding the news, imagining her life if she were married to Tina Fey, and the feeling of writing on a banana in biro.

Charity Blaine

Charity Blaine started making books at the age of seven, when her grade two teacher showed her how to sew together pages with thread and fashion a book cover from a recycled cereal box covered with construction paper. She continued this process independently into the third grade. In those days, all her stories ended with "and there was peace on earth" and centered on a little girl named Stephanie. Her characters are more varied these days, but most of her writing still focuses on peace, love, hope and happy endings. For a brief period, she wrote articles for her local newspaper and still contributes to various websites on occasion. She works as a photographer and information clerk at a public library in Ontario, Canada. She never stopped loving to write, and predominantly writes short stories, inspired by dreams and daily life, with a touch of magical realism. She can be found on instagram @alovelylittleworld or @lookingforearthstars

Chelsea Lewis

Chelsea "Rue" Lewis was just going to sign her name in tears but management advised her against intentional contribution to the mildewing of books. Rue is a humanoid shape composed of 60% fears and 40% tears. Sometimes those fears take shape and show up on sketchbook pages and tears form words that ought to be written down. She would like to contribute more in the alchemizing of others' words into figures on paper but for now Rue helps grow little seedling humans and teaches them to be brave and true. If you're curious you can observe the mess on Instagram at @chelsea.lew and @rueable.

Eileen Ramos

Eileen Ramos is a bipolar and queer Filipina American writer and bookseller. She is the Head Event and Donation Space Coordinator for The Asian American Literary Review's "Open in Emergency: A Special Issue on Asian American Mental Health" which is a multimedia book art project. She is also a proud member of GABRIELA New York which is a Filipina activist group. Her aforementioned crush enjoys her writing and wants to workshop together. She has decided that this is a better alternative to falling in love. It's more intimate anyway. You can find her on twitter/instagram at @eintervital. Her blog is vitalendeavor.wordpress.com.

Erin Kim

Erin Kim is an artist, writer, and everyday storyteller who often goes by Agnes. She's a personal essayist, singer songwriter, zine-maker, photographer, community manager and is launching her first print magazine of love letters, Lettres Mag (@lettresmag). She studied Media Storytelling at NYU Gallatin and made her photography debut sharing her self-portraits in local art galleries last year. She believes in self-empowerment, vulnerability as strength and using creativity to allow ourselves to find our individual truths. She'd love to be your friend @agnesonduty, erinkimnyc@gmail.com, and at www.erin.kim

Haley Littlefield

Haley Littlefield graduated from the University of Texas at Dallas with a B.A. in Literary Studies in 2013. During college and after graduation, she worked at a local library for six years until she left her position to spend more time on herself. She is married to a wonderful man (who definitely inspired her writing for this book) and they are raising a lovely daughter together. She enjoys cooking, doodling, reading, watching movies, riding her bike, and collecting cute mugs. She currently lives in Rowlett, Texas with her family and two cute dogs.

Kaitlyn Luckow

Kaitlyn is a photographer, writer, editor, and storyteller that is passionate about telling other people's stories in order to create empathy and understanding in this world. She is a freelance writer and editor as well as owns her own photography business with her husband, Alex. You can find her photography on Instagram @lykkevisuals and her writing @kaitlyn.luckow.

Lisa Wieczorek – p. 22, 34

Lisa is a designer, illustrator, artist, mess-maker, and bourbon enthusiast living in Chicago. She was born and raised there so she's prone to say strange things, like "frunchroom" instead of living room. She lives with her fluffy and sassy cat, Bowie, and her multitudes of plant babies. She started drawing at a very young age and loves dabbling in all different types of artistic and creative mediums. Her favorite is still drawing with ink and paper.

Lucy Ellerton

Lucy is an asthmatic, epileptic, blonde vegetarian, who is a recovering Candy Crush addict. No, she didn't just walk into a bar but she does like to write silly jokes and fun fiction. Lucy loves animals, loves kindness and she loves hearing ridiculous laughter (looking at you Jimmy Carr). She also loves everyone and everything in this compilation.

Meg Colt

Meg Colt is a freelance writer who candidly shares her experiences about her mental health. After going viral for blogging about her recovery from orthorexia, she began to share poetry and words in attempt to destigmatize society's stereotypes against those who struggle with mental illness. In her spare time she can be found chasing her children, cuddling cats, or drinking copious amounts of coffee. You can find her on Instagram: @meg_colt

Natalie Meagan

Natalie Meagan is an artist, occasional writer and founder of The Crybaby Club. She lives in Memphis, Tennessee with her two sons, Jack and Samson, and their dog, Cheese. She has been emotional and artistic for seemingly her entire life, and has since learned to combine those characteristics and use them to help spread message of female empowerment and crybaby pride to sensitive souls and empaths all over the world. It is her dream to meet and hug as many crybabies as she can in her lifetime, lead by example in supporting and lifting all women, and continue making a difference with her art.

Rebecca Foley

Rebecca has been writing since she was eight years old. One of the first pieces she can remember writing was a series of short mysteries about three detectives named Me, Myself, and I. Though she has moved past writing about Me, Myself, and I, she still looks back on those stories to remind her of how far she has come and where her love for writing began. At the age of 22, she had her first real experience with being published in Tough and Tender: Volume One. Now, 23, she is excited and proud to share her work once again, as well as, to be part of the editing team this time around. She recently graduated from Eastern Michigan University with a Bachelor's degree in Children's Literature. As a college graduate, she hopes to work in a library, while continuing to write. When she is not writing, she can be found surrounded by others' stories, whether it be through books, movies, or TV shows. She has always been fascinated by the story and hopes to one day have others fascinated and inspired by hers. Her writing style consists of mostly fiction in the prose form, but she has branched out into poetry. She has a wonderful family – a mom, dad, and older brother– who support her in all that she wants to accomplish. She would like to dedicate her writings to her late dog, Bailey, who passed away suddenly at the age of 11. She will be missed.

Rhea Smith

Rhea Smith, 25, has never quite fit any stereotype; but not for lack of trying. Student turned educator turned scientist turned writer/editor, she has dabbled in many hobbies and took quite nicely to spoken word and performing her writing aloud. She takes pride in her poetry, but also enjoys writing prose. When she's not spilling words on paper, she's likely singing them at the top of her lungs along with her guitar. Tough and Tender

Volume One marks the second anthology she has published, as writer, editor, and publisher - and now she is proud to present the third – Tough and Tender Volume Two. Rhea's other works can be found on her writing page at medium.com/@supernumerarysoul. Rhea also leads an indie writing collective titled Intrinsically Difficult, which can also be found on medium.

Rhianna Lesik

Rhianna is a creator who is passionate about photography, music, and exploring. She is a writer looking to start her career in poetry by sharing her poetry with others in the hopes of publishing her own collection. You can find her on Instagram @rhianna_lesik

Suzanna Valentine Moore

Suzanna Valentine Moore has been a lover of words all her life. Growing up in coastal Maine, in a literary haven, she dreamed of becoming a book editor when she was nine years old. To work towards her dream, she joined the Bank Street College Children's Book Committee where she was chosen to review books with intense subject matter. She reviewed Speak by Laurie Halse Anderson at twelve years old and she will never forget it. Fast forward eighteen years and Suzanna is still tackling heavy subjects in songwriting and non-fiction works. Her dream of becoming an editor swiftly changed over the years, but she continues to write every day. The Crybaby Club has inspired her to share her truth and strengthen her advocacy for human rights, mental health, and self-care. Suzanna is currently working on a self-care/love zine for her brand Little Pearl Naturals. Find her on Facebook and Instagram @LittlePearlNaturals. She resides in Fairfield, Iowa with her partner and their cat, Hyperbole.